MATH IT!
MEASURE IT!

by Nadia Higgins

pogo

Ideas for Parents and Teachers

Pogo Books let children practice reading informational text while introducing them to nonfiction features such as headings, labels, sidebars, maps, and diagrams, as well as a table of contents, glossary, and index.

Carefully leveled text with a strong photo match offers early fluent readers the support they need to succeed.

Before Reading

- "Walk" through the book and point out the various nonfiction features. Ask the student what purpose each feature serves.

- Look at the glossary together. Read and discuss the words.

Read the Book

- Have the child read the book independently.

- Invite him or her to list questions that arise from reading.

After Reading

- Discuss the child's questions. Talk about how he or she might find answers to those questions.

- Prompt the child to think more. Ask: Look around you. What do you see that you could measure?

Pogo Books are published by Jump!
5357 Penn Avenue South
Minneapolis, MN 55419
www.jumplibrary.com

Library of Congress Cataloging-in-Publication Data

Names: Higgins, Nadia, author.
Title: Measure it! / by Nadia Higgins.
Description: Minneapolis, MN: Jump!, Inc. [2016]
Series: Math it!
Audience: Ages 7-10.
Identifiers: LCCN 2016008867 (print)
LCCN 2016016181 (ebook)
ISBN 9781620314098 (hardcover: alk. paper)
ISBN 9781624964565 (ebook)
Subjects: LCSH: Measurement–Juvenile literature.
Classification: LCC QA465 .H54 2016 (print)
LCC QA465 (ebook) | DDC 530.8–dc23
LC record available at https://lccn.loc.gov/2016008867

Series Editor: Jenny Fretland VanVoorst
Series Designer: Anna Peterson
Photo Researcher: Anna Peterson

Photo Credits: Photo Credits: All photos by Shutterstock except: Getty, 5, 17, 18-19; iStock, 1, 14-15brm; Thinkstock, 10, 11, 12-13.

Printed in the United States of America at Corporate Graphics in North Mankato, Minnesota.

TABLE OF CONTENTS

CHAPTER 1
Will It Fit? 4

CHAPTER 2
Know Your Units 10

CHAPTER 3
Measure Smart 16

ACTIVITIES & TOOLS
Try This! 22
Glossary 23
Index 24
To Learn More 24

CHAPTER 1

. . . .

WILL IT FIT?

Who won the long jump?

Will the cake fit in the box without getting squished?

How much did you grow last year?

Get out your ruler! Measure to keep track of how things grow or to compare distances. Measure to see if something fits.

5 X 7 Inch Picture Frame

8 inches

5 inches

Will the picture fit in the frame? For this job, compare **height** and **width**.

The width looks OK, but not the height. How much will you have to cut off the picture to make it fit?

THINK ABOUT IT!

Imagine a world without measuring. There would be no recipes. No science experiments. Builders would have a terrible time making houses or furniture.

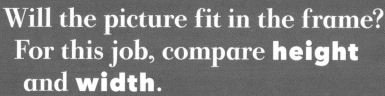

Josie the cat is going for a ride.
Is her carrier long enough?

Josie's size and the carrier's
size are too close to **estimate**.
You had better measure.

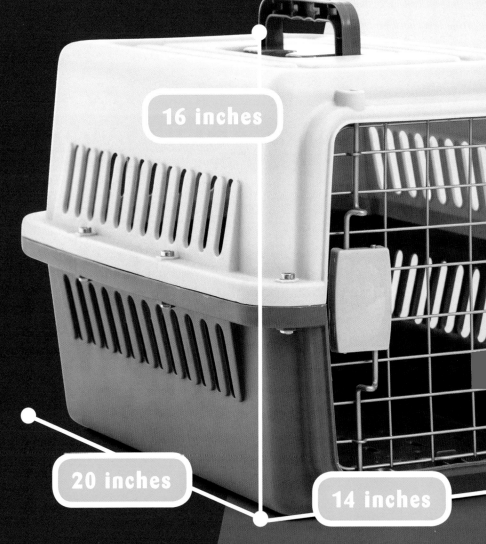

16 inches

20 inches

14 inches

The carrier's **length** is 20 inches. Josie is 15 inches long. Josie will fit with 5 inches left over. After all, she needs some space to wiggle.

15 inches

CHAPTER 2

KNOW YOUR UNITS

Ruby the parrot is 18 inches tall.

We could also say that Ruby is 1 foot, 6 inches.

Why?

36 inches = 3 feet = 1 yard

18 inches = 1½ feet

Because 1 foot has 12 inches.
12 inches + 6 inches = 18 inches,
Ruby's height.

Ruby's cage is 36 inches, or 3 feet,
tall. One yard equals 3 feet.

Now let's measure Ruby using the **metric system**. The metric system is a system of measurement used throughout the world. Instead of inches, use centimeters. Flip over your ruler. See the *cm*? That stands for centimeters. Your ruler measures both!

DID YOU KNOW?

Scientists prefer the metric system. Why? It is simple to switch from one **unit** to another. All units are in **multiples** of 10. For example, a meter equals 100 centimeters. That is a lot easier to remember than 12 inches in a foot and 3 feet in a yard.

centimeters · · · · ▶

Use a ruler or yardstick to measure some everyday objects. Now flip it over to measure using the metric system.

U.S. Quarter

1 inch wide
25 millimeters wide

School Bus

12 yards long
11 meters long

U.S. Penny

¾ inch wide
2 centimeters wide

U.S. Dollar

6 inches wide
15¼ centimeters wide

School Folder

1 foot long
30 centimeters long

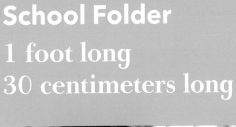

Milk Jug

9½ inches high
24 centimeters high

African Elephant

3¼ yards tall
3 meters tall

CHAPTER 3

MEASURE SMART

Make some measurements around your garden.

What units make the most sense for each item? Choose inches, feet, or yards.

how tall?

Now let's measure in metric. What items would you measure using centimeters? How about meters?

how long?

how wide?

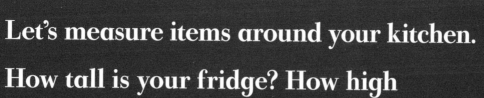

Let's measure items around your kitchen.

How tall is your fridge? How high is the countertop? How wide is your oven? How long are the sides of a cookie sheet?

TAKE A LOOK!

What is the best tool for each job? Choose a tool that is a little longer than what you are measuring.

RULER

A ruler shows 12 inches. The other side has 30 centimeters.

YARDSTICK

A yardstick goes up to 3 feet. It shows a meter on the other side.

TAPE MEASURE

A **tape measure** pulls out to several yards or meters. It can also bend around corners and curves.

Choose the best unit.
Choose the best tool.
The better you measure,
the more **precise** your
world will be!

ACTIVITIES & TOOLS

HUMAN RULERS

In ancient Egypt, people used their bodies to measure.
- One digit = the width of a finger.
- One palm = the width of four fingers.
- One span = the width of an open hand, from the tip of the thumb to the tip of the pinky.
- One cubit = the length from the elbow to the tip of the middle finger.

Let's see how well this system works for you and friend.

What You Need:
- a friend
- a ruler
- string
- scissors
- paper and pencil

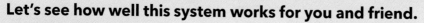

1. **Use a ruler to measure the width of one finger. That's 1 digit. Record your results in inches or centimeters. Do the same for 1 palm, 1 span, and 1 cubit. (See the chart above if you forgot what those are.)**

2. **Now help your friend collect his or her measurements.**

3. **How do the measurements compare? Do you see why the Egyptian system didn't last? More than likely, the answers are all over the place! That is why we have standard units today. An inch is always the same, no matter what ruler you use.**

GLOSSARY

estimate: To make a smart guess.

height: A measure of how high or tall something is.

length: A measure of how long something is, from end to end. Length is always greater than width.

metric system: A system of measurement used by most of the world. Centimeters and meters are units of the metric system.

multiples: Numbers that can be divided by other numbers without a remainder.

precise: Exact; not a guess.

tape measure: A long, flexible measuring tool. A tape measure often comes rolled up. You unroll it as far as you need.

unit: A fixed amount or length that is used to measure things. Inches and centimeters are units.

width: A measure of how wide something is, from side to side. Width is always shorter than length.

INDEX

centimeters 12, 14, 15, 17, 19

comparing 5, 7

distance 5

estimate 8

experiments 7

feet 10, 11, 12, 15, 16, 19

fit 4, 5, 7, 9

grow 4, 5

height 7, 10, 11, 18

inches 9, 10, 11, 12, 14, 15, 16, 19

length 8, 9, 14, 15, 18

meter 12, 14, 15, 17, 19

metric system 12, 14, 17, 20

millimeters 14

multiples 12

recipes 7

ruler 5, 12, 14, 19

tape measure 19

tool 19, 20

units 12, 16, 20

width 7, 14, 15, 18

yard 11, 12, 14, 15, 16, 19

yardstick 14, 19

TO LEARN MORE

Learning more is as easy as 1, 2, 3.

1) Go to www.factsurfer.com

2) Enter "measureit" into the search box.

3) Click the "Surf" button to see a list of websites.

With factsurfer, finding more information is just a click away.